For August, with much love. – Eric

To my mom, thanks for letting me be me.
I love you. – Jieting

First Edition
Kane Miller, A Division of EDC Publishing
Text copyright © Eric Ode 2021
Illustrations copyright © Jieting Chen 2021

For information contact:
Kane Miller, A Division of EDC Publishing
5402 S 122nd E Ave, Tulsa, OK 74146
**www.kanemiller.com**
**www.usbornebooksandmore.com**

Library of Congress Control Number: 2020948924

Manufactured by Regent Publishing Services
Hong Kong, China
Printed March 2021 in Shenzhen, Guangdong, China

ISBN: 978-1-68464-223-6

2 3 4 5 6 7 8 9 10

# STOP THAT POEM!

**Kane Miller**
A DIVISION OF EDC PUBLISHING

climb higher and higher

then settle like

birds on a wire

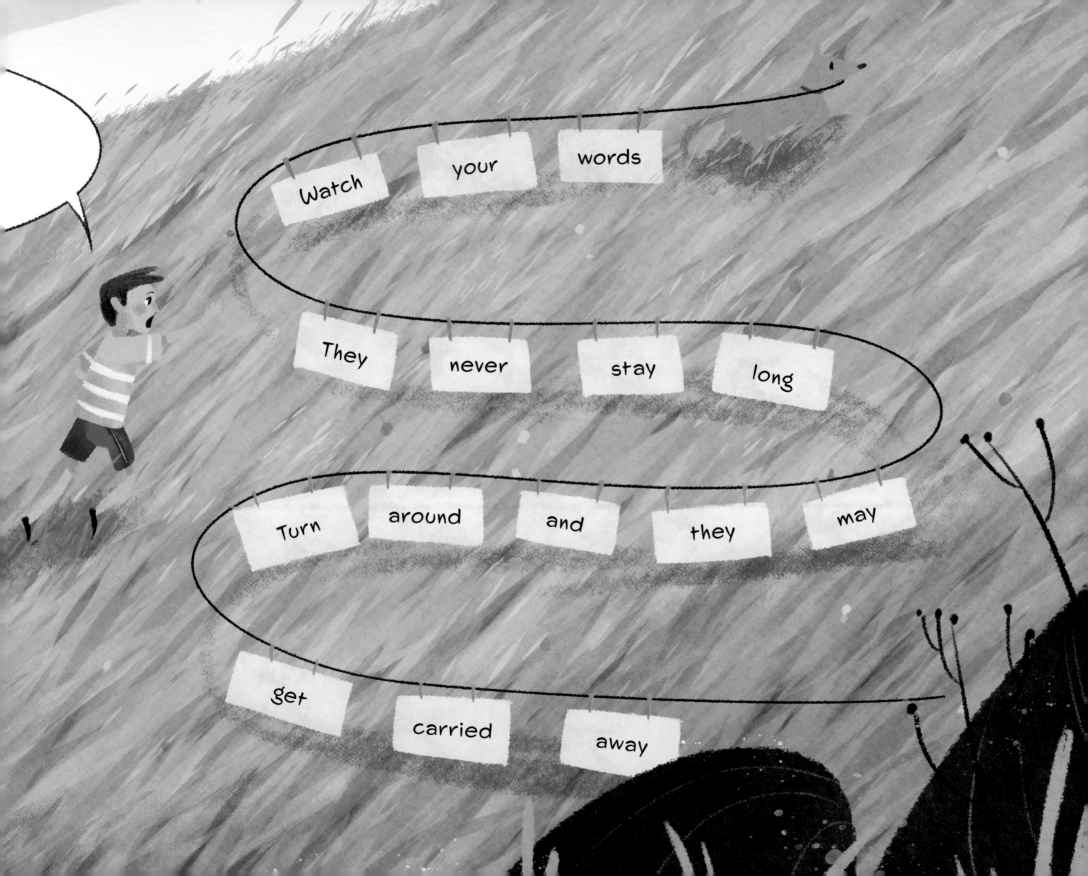

or rest like nests in the tall trees

They will rise like birds to reach

found

riding    on    a    noisy    bus

downtown

clattering chattering like a train

or scattering like pouring rain

Watch your poem grow

and climb

seed by seed

row by row

rhyme by rhyme